Seeds and Plants

Daisy Allyn

INFOMAX COMMON CORE READERS

Rosen Classroom™

New York

Published in 2013 by The Rosen Publishing Group, Inc.
29 East 21st Street, New York, NY 10010

Copyright © 2013 by The Rosen Publishing Group, Inc.

All rights reserved. No part of this book may be reproduced in any form without permission in writing from the publisher, except by a reviewer.

Book Design: Michael Harmon

Photo Credits: Cover (seeds and dirt) Bogdan Wankowicz/Shutterstock.com; cover (sky) Pakhnyushcha Shutterstock.com; p. 4 Marek Pawluczuk/Shutterstock.com; p. 5 Africa Studio/Shutterstock.com; p. 6 Urbanowicz/Shutterstock.com; p. 7 Mazzzur/Shutterstock.com; p. 8 matin/Shutterstock.com; p. 9 sunsetman/Shutterstock.com; p. 10 Martin Novak/Shutterstock.com; p. 11 visuall2/Shutterstock.com; p. 12 Bertl123/Shutterstock.com; p. 13 Iakov Kalinin/Shutterstock.com; p. 14 meirion matthias/Shutterstock.com; p. 15 (orange seeds) © iStockphoto.com/1001nights; p. 15 (oranges) holbox/Shutterstock.com; p. 15 (pumpkin seeds) Alekcey/Shutterstock.com; p. 15 (pumpkins) L.L.Masseth/Shutterstock.com; p. 15 (sunflower seeds) Sura Nualpradid/Shutterstock.com; p. 15 (sunflowers) Pakhnushcha/Shutterstock.com.

ISBN: 978-1-4488-8932-7
6-pack ISBN: 978-1-4488-8933-4

Manufactured in the United States of America

CPSIA Compliance Information: Batch #WS12RC: For further information contact Rosen Publishing, New York, New York at 1-800-237-9932.

Word Count: 113

Contents

Many Kinds of Plants 4

More Seeds and Plants 15

Words to Know 16

Index 16

There are many kinds of plants.

Most plants makes seeds.

The seeds grow into new plants.

Apple seeds grow inside apples.
They are small and brown.

Put an apple seed in the ground.

It will grow into an apple tree!

Peanuts are seeds.

They grow in a shell.

Some farmers plant peanuts.

The peanuts grow into peanut plants!

Acorns are seeds.

Acorns grow on oak trees.

Acorns fall from oak trees.
Some grow into new oak trees!

Coconuts are seeds.

They are the biggest seeds in the world!

Coconuts grow into coconut trees.

Coconut trees grow where it is sandy.

There are so many kinds of seeds.

Can you think of more seeds?

More Seeds and Plants

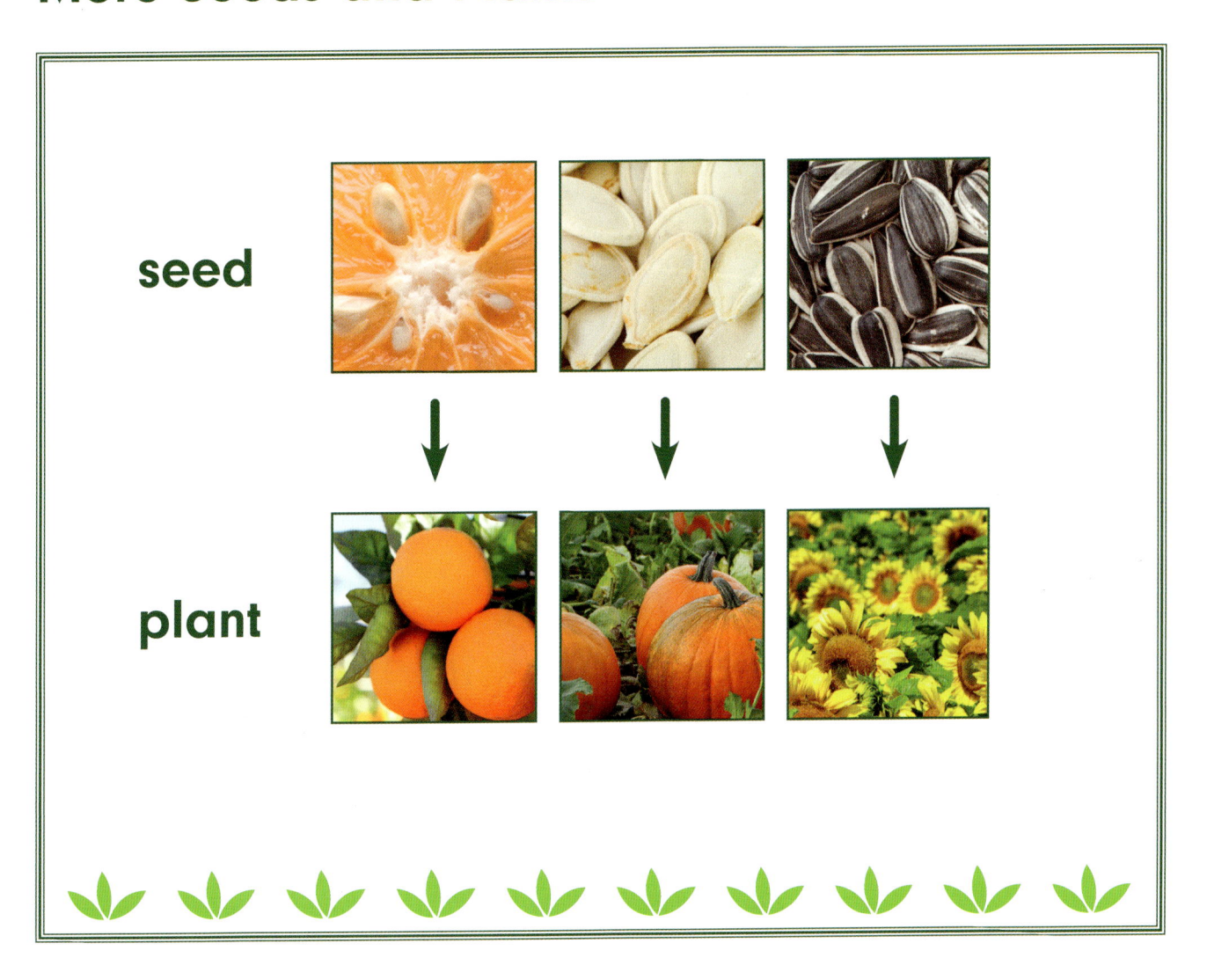

seed

plant

15

Words to Know

acorn

coconut

oak tree

peanut

shell

Index

acorns, 10, 11

apple(s), 6, 7

apple tree, 7

coconuts, 12, 13

coconut trees, 13

oak trees, 10, 11

peanut plants, 9

peanuts, 8, 9

plants, 4, 5, 15